W9-ACJ-996

MACCABEE JAMBOREE
A HANUKKAH COUNTDOWN

MACCABEE

A HANUKKAH

CHERI HOLLAND . . . . **PICTURES BY ROZ SCHANZER** . . . . . .

JAMBOREE
COUNTDOWN

KAR-BEN COPIES, INC. · ROCKVILLE, MD

To Jim, Sarah, Jacob, and Jesse
— CH

To Kim
—RS

Hanukkah celebrates the victory of the Maccabees, a small band of Jewish patriots, over the mighty armies of Syrian King Antiochus. When they restored the Holy Temple in Jerusalem, the Maccabees found one jar of pure oil, enough to keep the menorah burning for just one day. But a miracle happened, and the oil burned for eight days. Each night of the holiday, we light one more candle, exchange gifts, play dreidel, and eat potato pancakes and donuts to remember this victory for religious freedom and the miracle of the oil.

Library of Congress Cataloging-in-Publication Data

Holland, Cheri
Maccabee Jamboree: A Hanukkah Countdown / Cheri Holland : Illustrated by Roz Schanzer
p.   cm.
Summary: A counting book describing how the Maccabees have fun during the eight nights of Hanukkah, making cards, exchanging gifts, chanting blessings, and singing songs.
ISBN 1-58013-019-4
[1. Hanukkah — Fiction. 2. Jews — Fiction. 3. Counting.]
I. Schanzer, Rosalyn, ill. II. Title.
P27.H708213Mag 1998
[E] — dc21
98-4199
CIP
AC

Text copyright © 1998 by Cheri Holland
Illustrations copyright © 1998 by Roz Schanzer
All rights reserved. No portion of this book may be reproduced without the written permission of the publisher.
Published by KAR-BEN COPIES, INC., Rockville, MD 1-800-4-KARBEN (1-800-452-7236)
Printed in Mexico

It's time to celebrate the **8** nights of Hanukkah!

The Maccabees have lots of fun!

8 Maccabees made
Hanukkah cards.

But only **7** mailed them.

7 Maccabees twirled their dreidels.

But only **6** gathered their coins.

6 Maccabees exchanged gifts.

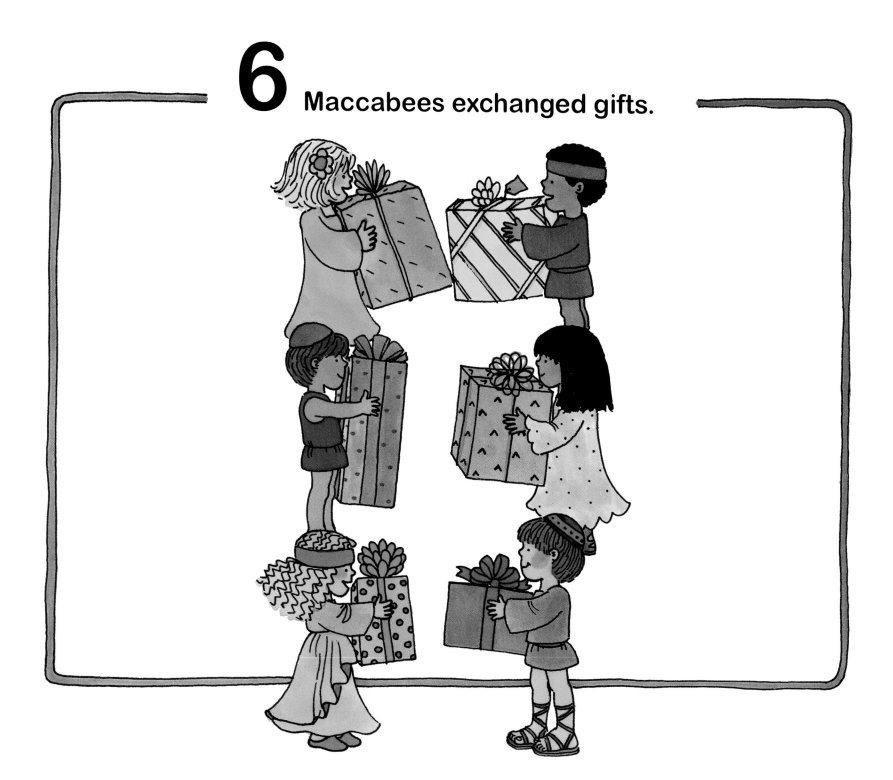

But only **5** unwrapped theirs.

5 Maccabees cooked latkes.

But only **4** gobbled them up.

4 Maccabees polished the menorah.

But only **3** put in the candles.

3 Maccabees sang Hanukkah songs.

But only **2** danced around.

2 Maccabees chanted the blessings.

But only **1** lit the candles.

1 Maccabee all alone,
wishing his friends were back.

Shhh!
Don't make
a sound!

So he danced around.

1 2 3 4 5 6 7 8

8 Maccabees all together again!